The Magic Chopsticks

Patricia Powell Pyne

Illustrations by Janet Lambert Moore

THE MAGIC CHOPSTICKS

Copyright © 1995 by Patricia Powell Pyne

Library of Congress 636-709
Internation Standard Book Number 0-9655465-9-4
Pelican Publishing Company, Lowell, Massachusetts
Sullivan Brothers Printers, Lowell, Massachusetts
Funded in part by the Lowell Cultural Council.

To the Leistikow Family

Enjoy !

Love,
Pat Lyne

Special thanks to Chinsan Lim.

Lowell, Massachusetts, has become the new home of thousands of Asian immigrants. This story is about one of them, a little Asian boy who suffers the loneliness of leaving the familiar to face a strange new culture, and how a wise teacher, and a little magic, help him find acceptance in his new land.

To the old mill city, where two rivers meet on their journey to the sea, Chen Lin and his family came from Asia, to start their new life in America.

Chen's sister, Janet, loved this exciting move, her new friends and school. But Chen was not happy. He felt lonely and sad.

Chen thought often about his old school, where he and his classmates, in identical uniforms, sat in straight rows and listened intently to Mr. Lee, their instructor. Everything was so different at the Riverview School.

His new teacher, Miss Carol, with her brown velvet eyes, laughed a lot with a big sunshiny smile. The children, all in different clothes, sat in groups. Chen felt very uncomfortable and alone.

In Chen's group sat Monique, who stared at him through big blue eyes. Blond Richard knew the answers to all of Miss Carol's questions.

Nancy, of the red curls and braces, always talked to him, but he didn't know some of the words, and felt too shy to answer her. Chen was miserable!

One Monday morning Miss Carol announced that Friday would be Around-the-World Food Day. All students would bring in a dish from their native land. Then Miss Carol called Chen to her desk and whispered in his ear.

Monique appeared on Friday with a beautiful quiche.

Richard staggered in carrying a huge bowl of Swedish meatballs.

Nancy was so excited about her hot Irish Bread.

Chen came in quietly with a huge covered tray.

Miss Carol told everyone to put their dishes on the big table. Then each student came up and explained about his or her native country, and told about the food.

When it was Chen's turn, he walked slowly to the table, spoke softly, and then lifted the cover.

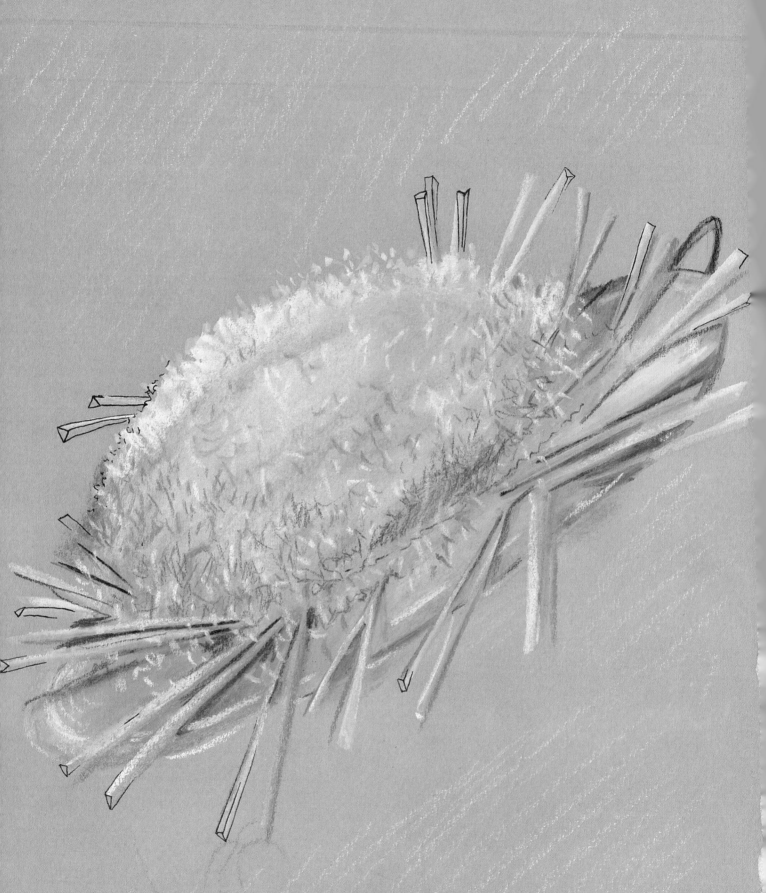

The tray was filled with rice and twenty-two pair of chopsticks!

The students got very excited as Chen demonstrated how to use the chopsticks!

Nancy shouted loudly, "Chen, eating tiny rice with these skinny sticks is like magic!"

Miss Carol smiled her sunshiny smile, and its sunshine spilled into Chen's heart, making it feel bright and warm. They both knew the chopsticks held more than rice. "Chen, you have made the class so happy by teaching us your wonderful custom!" Miss Carol exclaimed. "These are truly 'Magic Chopsticks'!"

The Magic Chopsticks held the promise of new friends and happiness for Chen in the old mill city where two rivers meet on their journey to the sea.

The End